09/19/12 QUICKREADS

WITHDRAWN
DANGER
ON ICE

JANET LORIMER

D1361995

SADDLEBACK
EDUCATIONAL PUBLISHING

▌QUICKREADS

SADDLEBACK
EDUCATIONAL PUBLISHING
www.sdlback.com

ISBN-13: 978-1-61651-179-1
ISBN-10: 1-61651-179-6
eBook: 978-1-60291-901-3

Printed in Guangzhou, China
0311/03-150-11

15 14 13 12 11   2 3 4 5 6

■ ■ ■

*C*an *you keep a secret?"*

Ken Hudson knew the voice was just in his head. He'd heard it before. Those words were left over from a nightmare he'd lived through six months ago. But for some reason the voice always surprised him—no matter how often it came back to haunt him.

Now, sitting across the desk from Dr. Grayson, Ken tried very hard to hide his discomfort. He certainly would never admit that he was hearing things.

The voice taunted him at the strangest times. Sometimes it whispered to him in bad dreams. Sometimes it echoed in his mind while he was awake. The words stuck like a sour odor that stays in your nose for a very long time.

Dr. Grayson looked up from Ken's résumé. "I see that you did a stint in the Marine Corps," he said as he raised one eyebrow and smiled.

Ken hated the man's smile. It was so *smug*. He swallowed back his irritation. "Yeah. I served for four years," he said.

"You were one of those famous 'few good men,' eh?" Sarcasm dripped from Grayson's words.

Ken's mouth tightened. "I like to think so, sir. We had a job to do and we were well-trained to do it."

Even Grayson couldn't miss the ice in Ken's tone. The older man's smile quickly faded, and he turned back to reading the résumé. "Then you worked for the police department—but you quit a month ago. Why?"

Ken paused for a moment to gather his thoughts. "There was—an incident. I—uh—I'd rather not go into the details. I just felt I needed to move on. That's why

I applied for this job."

Grayson gazed at Ken with open curiosity. He could see that the ex-cop had no intention of supplying those details. But Grayson couldn't stop digging. "Okay, tell me this," Grayson went on. "Did you lose your nerve? Would you be afraid to—"

Ken couldn't stop himself. He shot out of his chair and leaned close to Grayson's face. His eyes were narrow and his upper lip was drawn back. "Look, Dr. Grayson—I'm not afraid of anything. I assure you I can do the job! You want a security guard—I'm your man. You've got my references. If you don't believe me, why don't you talk to the people who know me?"

Grayson took a deep breath and leaned back in his chair. He gazed thoughtfully at Ken. "Very well," he said after a moment. "You do have good credentials, Hudson. And you're right, we need a man right away. Would you mind working the night shift?"

Ken shook his head.

"Then I guess you've got the job," Grayson

said. "My secretary will give you some forms to fill out. Oh, and she'll issue you a uniform." He stood up as if to dismiss Ken.

"Good enough," Ken said with a forced smile. He thought about shaking Grayson's hand, but changed his mind. Grayson was smooth, well-dressed, and well-educated. But something about the man made Ken's skin crawl.

■ ■ ■

One more thing," Grayson said, shuffling a stack of papers. Ken raised an eyebrow in question. "Are you licensed to carry a weapon?"

"I'll need a gun?" Ken asked.

Grayson looked uncomfortable. His glance didn't quite meet Ken's. "Uh—yes. Since you were a police officer, I thought—" his voice trailed away.

Ken nodded. "I'm licensed. Why?"

Grayson looked nervous now. He seemed to be choosing his words carefully. "Our company—CryoTech—is involved in some top-secret work. I suppose you know what it is we do?"

"Not exactly. Technology of some kind, but—" Ken shrugged. He felt a little silly not being able to answer.

Grayson smiled. "A *cutting-edge* technology," he said proudly. "We're researching cryonics." Ken hoped he didn't look as ignorant as he felt. Grayson motioned for him to sit down again. "Cryonics is about hope, Mr. Hudson. It's about the future. It's about offering people a chance at a new life."

Grayson stood and began to pace behind his desk. "Imagine that you come down with a fatal disease. You know that medical science is close to finding the cure—but you may not live long enough to reap the benefits. What if you could be frozen at the time of your death—and be kept that way? Then, when the cure was available, you could be brought back to life and treated." Grayson beamed. "You'd have a new life, Mr. Hudson!"

Ken stared at Grayson. He'd never heard of anything so weird.

Grayson saw the disbelief in Ken's eyes. The scientist's smile broadened. "Cryonics is not as crazy as you might think. There was the case of a child who fell through the ice on a frozen lake. When he was rescued, he showed no signs of life. Yet he was successfully thawed out and brought back to life—with no bad side effects. And he's a grown man now! What do you think of that?"

Ken took a deep breath and let it out slowly. He didn't know what to say.

"We have been able to lower the body temperature of laboratory mice until there were no signs of life at all. Then we thawed them out and brought them back to life."

Ken's skin broke out in a cold sweat. "So that's what you do here?" he asked. "You freeze living people—"

"*No!*" Grayson exclaimed. The question had clearly upset him. "That would be against the law—freezing someone who is still alive! We begin our special freezing process at the moment of death. Then the bodies are stored here for the future."

Ken felt extremely uncomfortable. He stared at Grayson in horror.

"You mean this place—"

"Yes, that's right," Grayson said cheerfully. "It's a storage facility. The building is full of bodies, all frozen. Our clients pay us a lot of money to care for their frozen bodies until the time comes for them to be thawed out."

"And have you done that?" Ken asked. "Have you successfully brought even *one* of these dead people back to life? Does your technology work?"

Grayson's face turned red, and he looked away. "Not yet—but there's no reason to assume it won't. That's why I say that CryoTech is all about hope!"

"Ah!" Ken nodded. He had begun to think that Grayson was just a nut case. On the other hand, the suit the scientist was wearing had cost a small fortune, and his office décor was elegant. Grayson had said it himself: People paid a lot of money for hope. "If this guy is crazy, he's crazy like a fox," Ken thought.

"I still don't understand why I need to carry a weapon," Ken said.

Grayson smiled coldly. "We're not the only company that does this kind of work, Mr. Hudson. We have secrets to protect from the competition."

The very idea of protecting dead people made Ken shudder.

■ ■ ■

Ken pulled up the collar of his jacket as he left the building. The sun was shining, but heaps of dirty snow were piled up in the shadows. The air was bitterly cold. Ken's breath rose in steamy plumes. He didn't know which was colder—the inside of the CryoTech facility or the chill air outside.

When he got to his car, he looked back just once. The shiny black building rose against a cold gray sky. CryoTech wasn't in a great location. It was close to the docks, next to the city's slums. By day, the area was dangerous enough. By night it would be even worse. Ken shivered as he climbed into his car. He was glad he'd be carrying a gun.

Ken knew he should go straight home. He needed to get some sleep before his shift started at midnight. Grayson had told him he'd be working with one other guard—Maggie Atkins. She'd be showing him the ropes.

Back in his apartment, Ken fixed himself a bowl of hot chili. He switched on the TV to catch some news while he ate. Halfway through his mid-afternoon lunch, the phone started ringing.

"Hey, buddy—you hear the news?" Ken recognized the gruff voice of his old partner, Nick Foley.

"Hey, Nick," Ken replied. "How's it going? What's up?"

"Leviathan," Foley said. "He's dead."

Ken froze. His enemy was *dead?* He couldn't believe it. "What happened?"

"Apparently he was killed last week," Nick said. "But it took the director of the prison mental hospital a few days to let us know. It seems a fight broke out among the inmates.

The word we got was that Leviathan was stabbed by one of the other prisoners."

Ken was silent for a moment. "Are you guys investigating?"

"Nope. It's out of our jurisdiction. Anyway, I thought you'd like to know. You should be able to sleep easier now."

"Thanks a lot," Ken said. But trying to imagine someone killing Leviathan was like imagining an elephant being killed by a bee sting.

"So how are things going with you?" Foley asked. "You find a job yet?"

Ken told Nick about his new job at CryoTech. "You ever hear of them?"

Foley said he hadn't. He wished Ken good luck and then said he had to go. But just as Ken was saying goodbye, he thought of something else. "Hey, Nick, did anyone—"

He heard the click as Nick hung up. "—see the body?" Ken went on, talking to no one. He replaced the receiver and sighed. "Someone from the department needs to I.D. that body," Ken thought. "Otherwise—"

Leviathan. That was the name the psycho serial killer called himself. The word meant "monster," and it described the guy perfectly. Leviathan was a huge man—nearly seven feet tall. He weighed a good 300 pounds, all muscle. Worst of all, he was far from stupid. In fact Leviathan held several college degrees. But he was also criminally insane.

For months on end, Leviathan had terrorized the city. The terrible crime scenes he'd left behind looked like slaughterhouses. Leviathan always carved up his victims like sides of beef.

In an effort to smoke out the monster, Ken had grown desperate. He had publicly made fun of the killer on TV. It had worked almost *too* well. Leviathan had sworn revenge and come after him.

One dark night in a big, deserted warehouse near the docks, Ken had accidentally walked into Leviathan's trap. It was too late when he realized what he had done. Leviathan grabbed him in a stranglehold and put his lips next to Ken's ear. The cop smelled the sour stench of decay and death.

"Can you keep a secret?" Leviathan had laughed, a maniac screech that tore open the night. *"I'm going to live forever."*

The killer's fingers dug into Ken's throat. As he fought for breath, pain exploded in every part of Ken's body. Leviathan wouldn't let him breathe. Ken was on the far edge of consciousness when he'd heard shots being fired. Then everything went black.

Later, after he came to, Ken learned that Leviathan was still alive. They said he'd been locked away in a prison hospital for the criminally insane.

■ ■ ■

I'm going to live forever!" That was when the nightmares had started. Ken struggled to get over them by working with the police department psychiatrist. But it did no good. Almost every night, he and Leviathan tangled again in his tortured dreams. Night after night he woke up screaming, Leviathan's horrifying secret echoing in his head. "I'm going to live forever!"

"But now he's dead," Ken thought to himself, as he carried his bowl to the sink. Again he said the words out loud. Leviathan is dead. But somehow the statement rang false. It sounded flat and unconvincing in the silent room.

Ken had told Grayson that he wasn't afraid of anything. But he had lied. Deep down inside, Ken was terrified of Leviathan—alive or dead.

■ ■ ■

About 15 minutes before midnight, Ken parked in the lot outside the CryoTech building. As he walked across the empty lot, a freezing wind whipped at his collar. Just inside the glass door at the entrance, he saw a dark figure watching his approach. Maggie Atkins?

Before she'd let him in, the female security guard insisted on seeing his I.D. badge. Ken was grateful for her caution. It would be good to be working with a real professional again.

Once Ken got inside, Maggie introduced herself. She was a tiny woman with blond hair and brown eyes, but Ken didn't doubt Maggie's ability. "She's a fifth-degree black belt," Grayson had told him. "She can disarm you faster than you can say hello."

Maggie wasted no time on polite chatter. "I'll go over the routine only once, Hudson. It's up to you to remember everything. This is the reception area."

Ken gazed about as Maggie talked. On the left, doors led to the offices of the CryoTech executives. On the right was a set of double doors that led to the storage facility. "That's where the clients are held," she said.

Ken drew a deep breath. *"Clients?* You mean the dead people?"

Maggie grinned. "We're supposed to call them clients. Grayson and the others want to think that they aren't really dead. They're in suspension."

"Do you really believe they can be brought back to life?" Ken asked.

Maggie shrugged. "It doesn't matter what

you and I think. We have a job to do. We patrol the building, watch for signs of anyone trying to break in. We keep an eye on the equipment, too."

She pulled open one of the double doors and gestured for Ken to enter.

He was surprised by what he saw. The giant room held nothing but glass and metal tanks standing upright. Hoses and wires attached each tank to refrigeration machinery. Inside each tank was what looked like a body bag suspended in some kind of liquid.

"Liquid nitrogen," Maggie explained. "It's maintained at several hundred degrees below freezing."

Ken blew on his fingers and made a mental note to wear gloves in the future. "So this is it?" he asked.

"There are doors at the back of the facility," Maggie said. "They lead to a loading dock. That's where the new clients arrive. We check to make sure the doors are locked. We patrol the offices and reception area. And we keep an eye on the storage tanks—just in case."

"Have you ever had a tank leak or break?" Ken asked.

"No," Maggie said, "although—" She bit back her words.

Ken frowned. "Although *what?* Come on, Atkins, you need to fill me in."

"Oh, nothing. It's just that this place can give you the creeps. I consider myself a fairly levelheaded person. But after you've patrolled CryoTech for awhile—" Her voice faded, and she shivered.

By now they had reached the end of the first row of storage tanks. Ken noticed a door painted bright red. The words *NO ADMITTANCE* were printed across it in large black letters.

Ken stopped in front of the door. "Where does that lead?" he asked.

"That's the laboratory," Maggie said. "As you see, it's off-limits to us, Hudson. We stay out of there."

"Then who checks it?"

Maggie shrugged. "It doesn't get checked. That's where the doctors do their top-secret experiments."

"What experiments?" Ken asked.

"I suspect they're trying to bring frozen bodies back to life," Maggie said.

"You look suspicious, but what's wrong with that?" Ken asked. "Isn't that what cryonics is all about?"

Maggie stopped and gazed at Ken. "Think about it, buddy. If you paid a million bucks to have yourself frozen so that someday you could be cured—"

Ken's stunned whistle cut her off. "That's a lot of money."

"They can't experiment with the paying clients, right?" Maggie went on. "So I've been wondering who or what they're experimenting on in there."

"Okay," Ken said. "I give up. Who—"

Maggie cut him off. "The thing is, I've seen some pretty weird stuff here." She glanced nervously from side to side. "Near the lab there's a special section of tanks with no nametags. Sometimes there are some body bags in the tanks, and sometimes there aren't."

All of a sudden, Ken remembered something he'd read about grave robbers. In the early 1800s, doctors needed to study human bodies to learn more about health and disease. But they weren't legally allowed to dissect the dead. So some doctors paid grave robbers to dig up fresh corpses for their experiments. Now and then, when the grave robbers couldn't find a fresh corpse, they became desperate. A few of them ended up committing murder.

"And—" Maggie stopped abruptly. "One night I heard—" She gazed at Ken nervously. "No—you'll think I'm nuts."

"No, I won't," Ken said. "Come on, Atkins. You have to tell me."

"It sounded like a voice."

"In the lab?" Ken asked. That was easily explained away. He was surprised Maggie would let herself get so spooked.

"It came from *inside* the tank," she

whispered, *"and it was screaming!"*

■ ■ ■

As the rest of the week went by, Ken grew more familiar with CryoTech's facility. His routine duties became automatic, and he stopped tensing at every strange noise when he patrolled. The storage tanks and their gruesome contents became a normal part of the scenery. Ken began to relax.

One night, Dr. Grayson and his team arrived after midnight. Ken let them in the back door, wondering what had brought them to the facility so late. "Is anything wrong?" he asked, as the scientists hurried into the laboratory.

Dr. Grayson glared in Ken's direction. "Everything's just fine as far as *you're* concerned!" he snarled.

The red door slammed shut behind him. Shocked at the man's rudeness, Ken swore quietly under his breath.

Maggie heard him and laughed. "Once old Grayson no longer needs to impress you, it's goodbye Mr. Charm," she explained with a grin.

Ken gave a mock shudder. "No kidding. What do you think is going on in there, Maggie?"

She shrugged. "We humble security guards are never given that information. But CryoTech hasn't received any new clients for a few days. I'm guessing that they must be conducting another experiment."

A few hours later, the CryoTech scientists emerged from their lab. They looked exhausted.

Ken followed them to the back door, then locked it after the team had left. He glanced at his watch. It was almost three in the morning. Five more hours and he could go home.

As he returned to the front of the storage room, he suddenly shivered.

Maggie saw it. "I'm glad I'm not the only one who's feeling—"

She stopped abruptly. Ken glanced at her, one eyebrow raised questioningly.

"Call it intuition," Maggie said, lowering

her voice. "But something's *wrong* here. I just don't know what."

Ken checked to see that his gun would slide out of its holster easily.

"Listen," Maggie said quietly. "Let's double-check all the offices and the reception area. You know—just to be on the safe side."

Ken nodded. He, too, was feeling a little uneasy. But *why?* He couldn't put his finger on it.

The moment they left the storage area, the uneasy feeling went away. After checking the rest of the building, they returned to their guardpost.

As they walked toward the red door, Ken and Maggie looked at each other. "I wish Grayson would install a security camera in the lab," Ken complained. "It would make our job a lot easier."

"I suggested it," Maggie said. "But Grayson refused. He said that their work is classified top-secret."

Ken started to reply, but suddenly both he and Maggie heard a series of strange noises coming from behind the red door. They froze.

"Hear that?" Maggie whispered. Her right hand moved toward her holster.

Ken nodded. They waited. Silence.

"Maybe one of the doctors came back for something," Ken said. "Don't they have keys to the back door?"

Maggie thought about that for a moment. "Grayson has keys, but—"

The sounds were repeated. Then the laboratory door shook as if something had struck it from the inside.

Maggie and Ken crouched, pulling their weapons free. Ken signaled to Maggie that he was going to move closer. She nodded, creeping into a defensive position on the other side of the door.

■ ■ ■

All of a sudden, the entire door broke loose and crashed to the floor. Ken stared, horrified. He simply couldn't believe what he saw. Leviathan was *alive*—and he was in the doorway!

The man looked like something from a bad horror movie. His features were bloated. His skin was blotched an ugly purplish-green. His lips were drawn back over stained and broken teeth. But the terrible insanity in his eyes was the same as ever.

As Ken gazed in disbelief at his enemy, Maggie raised her gun and took aim. Ken wanted to cry out, to warn her, but his vocal cords refused to work.

Leviathan spotted Maggie, and in one giant stride, he was on her. He quickly snatched her gun, flinging it aside like a plastic toy. His other hand gripped her arm.

Then Leviathan lifted her into the air, and Maggie cried out in surprise. She dangled as helplessly as a rag doll.

Her cry brought Ken back to life. He dropped to one knee, raised his gun with both hands, and took careful aim. Should he shoot? He didn't want to hit Maggie, but he *had* to disable the monster.

When Leviathan noticed Ken, recognition flashed in his eyes. He grinned as he waved

Maggie back and forth in front of him. Ken pulled back his gun.

Maggie saw her chance and kicked out hard, hitting Leviathan in the stomach. The blow took the man's breath away. When his grip loosened, Maggie wriggled free and fell to the floor. Before the monster could grab her again, Ken raised his gun and fired.

The bullet struck Leviathan in the shoulder. Something dark and inky spurted from the wound. Ken blinked in surprise. *It didn't look like blood.*

The wound didn't stop the monster for long. Leviathan reached for Maggie, but she quickly moved out of his reach. Ken grabbed her arm, pulling her next to him. He knew they had very little time, but he had a plan that just might work! When he whispered hoarsely in Maggie's ear, her eyes widened, but she nodded in agreement.

The enraged giant lumbered toward them, but Maggie scuttled away, staying just out of reach. "Hey, Mr. Ugly," she taunted. "I hear you think you're hot stuff with the ladies."

Leviathan's gaze followed her. His insane grin widened as Maggie continued insulting him. Leviathan moved closer to her. Ken winced as she danced back and forth, tossing insults at the killer. "Stay out of reach, Maggie," he hissed.

Positioning himself just behind Leviathan, Ken glanced around desperately. A second later, he spotted what he needed— a shiny steel scalpel. Ken grabbed it, careful not to touch the razor-sharp blade. He stepped into the monster's line of sight.

But Leviathan seemed to have forgotten about Ken. His attention was focused on Maggie, who was backing toward the empty tanks. Oh, no! Ken saw that she would soon be trapped. If he didn't act quickly—

■ ■ ■

Suddenly, Maggie bumped up against the nearest tank. Her eyes widened when she realized that she couldn't go any farther. Leviathan stepped into her path and closed in. His hands were reaching for her throat when Ken leaped. He struck the monster from behind, pushing the brute off balance. Maggie slipped away just as Leviathan staggered forward, lost his balance, and fell heavily against the tank.

The monster was dazed by the blow to his head. Leaping up, Ken raised the scalpel and stabbed Leviathan in the back of the neck. *"Now,* Maggie!" Ken yelled, pushing himself off the killer.

She fired into the glass tank. As it shattered, hundreds of gallons of liquid nitrogen flooded over Leviathan. The chemical drenched the wounds on the back of the giant's neck. Within seconds, his spinal cord was frozen. Ken and Maggie heard garbled screams as the giant twitched violently. Then he collapsed and was silent.

■ ■ ■

*C*an you keep a secret?"

Ken forced himself to ignore the ghostly voice he kept hearing in his head. Instead, he tried to focus on what Nick Foley was saying.

"It turns out the prison hospital was running a nasty little side business," Foley growled. "When they had a spare body—say, after a fight—some of the attendants sold it to CryoTech."

Ken shuddered. "So that's where Cryo-Tech was getting all the new guinea pigs for their experiments!"

Nick shifted in his chair. "It's still not clear if *all* the guinea pigs were dead when the CryoTech scientists picked them up. It's possible that—"

But Ken wasn't really listening.

"Looks like Maggie and I are out of a job," he said. "I don't suppose—" He smiled hopefully.

Nick grinned back. "The chief is going to call you tomorrow. You guys are going to be offered juicy positions with the department. The only problem is that I have a new partner now, and—" He looked uncomfortable.

"That's okay," Ken laughed. "*I* have a new partner, too." After what he and Maggie had been through at CryoTech, Ken was glad that the two of them might go on working together.

"Tell me again," Ken asked. "What actually happened to Leviathan's body?"

Nick stared at Ken in disbelief. "How many times do we have to spell it out for you, Hudson? He's *dead!*"

"Yeah, right. That's what you said last time," Ken said with a grin.

Nick laughed. "Okay, okay. Well, this time he really *is* dead."

Still smiling, Ken nodded. But right then and there he made a mental note to be sure that his gun was always kept clean and loaded.

It wasn't likely that he would ever forget what Leviathan had told him: *"I'm going to live forever!"*

After-Reading Wrap-Up

1. Think of another exciting title for *Danger on Ice.*

2. Name three things about Leviathan that make him a frightening and dangerous villain.

3. Did you hope Ken would come out a winner in this story? Why or why not?

4. Who would you rather have as a boss— Dr. Grayson or Maggie? Explain your answer.

5. When a scene is suspenseful, you don't know how the problem or situation is going to come out. Think about a suspenseful scene from another book you've read or a movie you've seen. Describe it.

6. Reread the pages about Maggie and Ken's battle with Leviathan. How does the author make this scene interesting to read? Give details in your explanation.

[8]